The author was born in the West Midlands; left school without any exams to his name. After leaving school, he worked in two day-centres doing different jobs from a canteen assistant to a wood-worker.

In his late seventies, he'd worked as a bingo caller in a bingo hall. The author doesn't wish to reveal his real name at this time.

I want to dedicate this book to four favourite authors who are Arthur Conan Doyle the author of *Sherlock*, Ruth Rendell, author of a book called *The Thief*, Colin Dexter, the author of *Inspector Morse* and Agatha Christie for *Hercules Poirot and Miss Marple*; these books and films have been beneficial to me in my writing career.

Eugene Pike

THE CRIME COLLECTION

AUSTIN MACAULEY PUBLISHERS™

LONDON • CAMBRIDGE • NEW YORK • SHARJAH

A CIP catalogue record for this title is available from the British Library.

ISBN 9781528977951 (Paperback)
ISBN 9781528977975 (ePub e-book)

www.austinmacauley.com

First Published (2020)
Austin Macauley Publishers Ltd
25 Canada Square
Canary Wharf
London
E14 5LQ

I want to thank the City of Wolverhampton College for their English courses and the WEA for their creative writing course that's been a great help to me. Also BBC and ITV for their crime series that have helped me with the ideas for my stories. I hope that one of them will show mine someday.

The Gunman in Black

'On a cold December afternoon in 1970, Benny Holland sat at his desk at 347, Dubbing Street, Benson: a small village town in the West Midlands.

He was smoking a rolled-up cigarette, at about two in the afternoon; his telephone rang; he picked it up and spoke to a four-foot-tall, blonde woman with pale green eyes.

She sat in her office in the bath opposite to his, drinking a can of beer. He gazed through the office window and saw a shadowy figure standing in the doorway in the shape of a five-foot-tall woman with red hair; she knocked on his door.

His ex-wife Jackie stood outside his office door, in just a short dressing gown. Underneath it, she had nothing 'on'.

Benny saw Jackie standing there; she said, "I'll just go and put some clothes on."

Benny just stared at her and said, "Don't mind me. I like girls in short dressing-gowns, no concealed weapons."

'He walked to the door, opened it and yelled,
"Come in."

Mrs England entered the office; she's dressed in a long, dark-red coat with matching trouser. On her head, she wore a Muslim woman's scarf and dark glasses. She introduced herself to him and spoke, "Hi, I'm Mrs England. I want to hire you to look for my son Harold."

She lived a simple life and hardly spent little of her money apart from holidays with the family.

He wrote down the details on a pad he'd taken from his desk. From his shirt pocket, he removed a pack of players' cigarettes, sitting there with his feet on the counter.

He spoke, "The price is £200 a day, plus expenses, I work alone; 'no police involvement. When did you last see your son?"

"Two weeks ago, when he left the house for school, and he didn't return home, later that afternoon, I received this note in the mail asking for money," she handed him the note. He read it; the letter said, "£ 10.000 or you won't see your son alive again."

"Do you know who sent the note, did you pay it? And have you been to the school and asked them if they know when he went?"

"I've no idea who sent the note. No, I've not paid. I jumped into my car and drove to the docks."

"What did you find when you got there?"

"Nothing, there was no-one there."

On her departure from his office, his telephone rang again, he walked around the other side of the desk and picked up the receiver. Jackie mumbled,

"Hello, darling, it's Jackie here."

"What can I do for you now?"

"Two police officers are on their way to your office, to arrest you."

"For what?"

"For fraud."

"What fraud?" he asked.

"Back when you used your friend's name."

"Oh, that."

"Yes, that."

Det Ch Inspector Des Ashwood and DS Kevin Jessup, two Asian fraud Instigates, hammered on his door as if their lives depended on it.

They shouted, "Mr Holland, open the door, we'd like to come in, and we'd like a word with you, sir!"

He just sat there, staring through the glass in the door, slamming down the receiver and thought of the woman who had just left his office and the case he'd been working 'on.

Later that day, he left his office, entered his Aston Martin DB5 and drove to the docks. There he came across four sailors who roughed him up, and they asked him what he'd wanted with them.

"Who are you looking for, pal?"

His reply was,

"I'm looking for Harold England."

"You won't find him here!" replied Wayne Jennings, the head gangster: a furry years old, six-foot-tall whitish male with black hair, clean-shaven.

Benny fought back with a Kung Fu kick, knocking them out cold.

He managed to drag himself back to his car and cleaned himself up. He found a bar and entered.

Behind the bar stood a black female named Karen Lawton, she wore a navy-blue T-shirt with black slacks, wearing a pair of gold-rimmed specs. Benny sat at the bar and ordered a beer. He spoke to her about the case he's working on and asked her where he could find the missing boy.

She replied, "I just work here and serve drinks, sir."

Benny threw down a twenty-pound note onto the bar. Karen reached for it, but he stopped her by placing his hand over hers and said,

"I only pay you if you tell me where I can find Harold England."

She picked up a beer mat and wrote the address on the back. 'This was a derelict housing estate. 'After he left the bar, he drove to the address, looked around and there he found the boy next to the body of a dead woman. Her body was lying in a pool of blood.

She'd been shot twice through the back of the head. He thought to himself, *Who was the dead woman? What have I uncovered? Could this be the work of Joseph Wagner, the Mafia boss, who was behind all those gangland killings, all those years ago? Wasn't he killed?*

It was past ten when they found Joseph's body slumped across the front seat of his car in Benson. He was found dead on May 23, 1975.

The verdict was that he killed himself due to depression, a witness said his people had killed him to stop him from giving evidence, droning the Second World War he'd served in the RAF, as a fighter pilot.

As he rescued the boy, a white Jaguar with black windows started shooting at him.

He couldn't see the driver, but the driver could see him. He fired back, hitting the fuel tank that exploded and killing the person with it, or so he thought.

He stopped and parked his car on the bridge and left it there. He left his car and walked over to the other side of the bridge.

'This was the only way out. All he found in the car was a badge with the name of Glenda Maxwell. He couldn't talk to the police because of his criminal record.

In the back of the other car, he found a body of 17-year-old Lindsey Wilson; she was very close to criminals of the underworld.

She would blackmail her friends to get money out of the, and if they didn't give it to her, she'd send the mafia boys around to see them, and they 'were killed for not giving her the money.

"Who was she?" he looked through the boot of the burnt-out car, where he discovered a silver steel case. Carrying the suitcase to his car, he placed it on the bonnet and opened it.

Inside were a rifle, money, and the badge with Glenda Maxwell's name on it.

"Did this belong to the dead girl in the car?"

He held it in his right hand, as he turned it over, there on the back, he found an address of an escort club called 'Alex'.

It was one of those clubs where men went for sex. After midnight, Benny visited this club to speak to the owner, Galaxy May Richardson, moved into the sex and protection business, and if people failed to pay her, they were shot dead. She was very friendly with criminals.

Benny walked in and sat at the bar. That night, there was a lot of gaming going on; 'games like blackjack and roulette. While this was going on, in the back-room, a man and woman were having sex.

Freddie the barman, an ex-boxing promoter, asked Benny,

"How can I help you, sir?"

He said, "I'd like to speak to Miss Richardson about a body I found."

"What body?"

"Miss Wallison's, she was only seventeen."

"Was she? Would you like a drink while you wait, sir?"

"No, thank you! I'll sit here and wait if you not mind."

"I don't mind sir; I just work here."

"Is Miss Richardson in?"

"She's in the back dealing with one of her girls."

"Why? What's the girl done?"

"She was caught stealing money from a client, who she was entrancing."

"What's going to happen to her? Is she going to be killed?"

"No, not this time sir, she's going to be spanked over Miss Richardson's knee."

"Oh, yes! I forgot that Miss Richardson smacked her girls' backsides when they do wrong dune's she? Things that go on behind closed doors ha."

Benny couldn't wait any longer. He got up off the barstool and walked to the door on to the street, crossed over the road and jumped into his car and drove back to his office.

He thought of the dead woman, "Could she be the assassin, could this be her identity?" On her body, he found a letter that told him that the boy was born 13 years ago after he left the force. He thought to himself, *could he be my son? She never told me that he was mine; all those years she kept this to herself, why?*

On returning to his office, he sat at his desk and poured himself a cup of coffee. After two sips of the coffee, he passed out on the office floor. Awoke an hour later to find a gunman standing over him.

The gunman was dressed in a long black coat that came down to his shoes and on his head. He wore a black biker helmet that covered his face. Benny grabbed the gun, wrestling with him around the floor and it went off, killing the man in black.

His thoughts were: *What can I do? I must dispose of the body before the police find it.*

He placed the body in the back of his car and drove to an incinerator. He stopped the car and put the gunman's body into it.

Re-entered his car and drove back to his office, parked it, got out, walked across the road and in through the glass doors and claimed the stairs to his private office. He pushed the door open he walked over to the desk and sat in the chair with his feet up, smoking a cigarette.

He looked through the newspaper that was on the desk. He just sat there with a smile on his face, switched on the radio for Radio 3, for the news and to listen to 'Mozart's opera' and threw some clothes into his tatty old case, switched his mind off the terrestrial troubles that went on around him. So, this helped him to forget what just happened.

He was about to pick up the receiver to speak to Jackie when two of the Jennings' boys kicked on his door. He slowly pulled the desk drawer out, taking from there, a Smith & Wesson .38 special and shot at the glass.

He hit the first man in the arm, who rolled down a flight of stairs and fell out of the window. CRASH! Jackie heard the commotion and came out of her office. From her handbag, she took out a silver pearl-handled pistol.

She aimed it through the crack of the door and fired, wounding the other man in the arm, who fell over the railing and landed on the floor at the bottom of the stairs.

Benny limped down the stairs, picked up the body of Bobby Jennings, a 34-year-old six-foot-tall male with short, black hair; 'a bearded man, who wore brown NHS spectacles that he removed.

Carried Jennings' body to his car, he placed it on the back seat, drove to the cliff, moved the body to the front seat and pushed the car over; that it exploded.

He walked back to the road and jumped into a yellow taxicab that was waiting there, "Where to?" the cab driver asked.

"To 347, Duping Street and step on it."

He sat back on the seat, as the taxicab reached 30mph, it exploded, but he was thrown clear. He rocked down the bank, got up and walked across the road in through the back door.

He entered the lift, pressed the button to the second floor the door opened, limping back to his office, he saw a light; on'.

"Who's in there and who's this?"

Benny walked across the hallway to his office, with his left foot, pushed the door open; walked in and hesitated, "Who could this be...?" he asked himself, "No-one comes to see me."

As he opened the door, they're sitting at his desk, was his ex-partner, Sandy Stafford. She, too, was an ex-police officer who 'was also thrown out because of her sexual fantasies with her boss.

She 'was caught lying across his desk with her underwear down, 'being smacked on her backside with a cane.

"Hey, you're sitting in my chair."

He walked over to the drinks cabinet, reached for the bottle of Johnnie Walker; into a glass, he poured himself a small measure.

"Fancy one? What can I do for you, madam?"

"I've heard you're a PI."

"I'd like you to work for me."

"Doing what?"

"Help me get my job back."

"Why should I help you? What's in it for me?"

"I can pay you."

"I don't work for family or friends."

He sipped his scotch, and from his desk drawer, he removed a packet of cigarettes, took one from the box, placed it into his mouth, struck a match on his thumb and lit it.

He offered her one, she took a cigarette from the box and placed it into her mouth, lighting it, she puffed on it and started to sweat.

"I'll open the window."

As he attempted this, she became drowsy and passed out on the floor of his office. Benny tried to revive her, but she was dead.

He dragged her body into a downstairs room in the basement, left it there and locked it in.

He walked back up the stairs to his office, picked up the cigarette and sniffed it, "Cyanide."

Outside, he heard the sound of a car revving up with the left hand. He looked through the blinds and caught glided of the number plate that was L76 on a silver-grey Citroen car.

Benny climbed out of his office window, limped down the fire escape and went off in hot pursuit of the grey limousine.

He had them cornered in an old scrapyard, where they had a gun battle. Benny hit the fuel tanker that exploded; the gangsters fired back, hitting Benny in the chest.

He crawled behind the back of the car, checking his gun.

"Three bullets left," he said to himself, after removing one of them and looked around for a way out.

On the ground beside him was an old grenade. He knelt and picked it up. Unscrewing the cap from the bullet, he poured the powder into the shell, sticking two matchsticks into it.

He fastened it to the other fuel tank which exploded, killing Watford and Turner – the two gangsters.

Benny jumped into the car and crashed through the gate of the hospital and died on the floor from the bullet wound.

Or did he?

'It was eight o'clock the next morning when Doctor A. Fleming came on duty and found a body. She walked over to the desk and said, "I need some help here, please." Two young doctors came to her aid. They placed the body onto a trolley and weaned it into the medical room. They tried saving him and worked around the clock.

After some time, Doctor Fleming said, "OK, stop, he's dead." 'She took a pen from her pocket and wrote down his name on the chart next to her, B Holland. But was it?

"Time of death: three o' eight, on July the sixth."

She looked through the pocket of the person's jacket. There she found a card with the name of Benny's ex-wife, Jackie.

She walked over to her desk, picked up the phone and dialled the number. It rang for some time, then a woman's voice spoke.

"Hello, who's this?"

"I'm Doctor Fleming. I'm calling from the hospital about Mr B Holland."

"Why, what's the matter with him?"

"He's dead."

"Is he?"

"What kind of job did he do?"

"He was some the licensed investigator, Detective."

"A bit of a Sherlock Holmes, was he?"

"No, he wasn't that good. He didn't get many cases."

'It was like something from a Greek tragedy."

The doctor walked to her office and filled out the form. The clock on the wall struck six. His ex-wife, dark-eyes, sturdily small, strong faced woman, came through the backdoor.

In her early thirties, with thick black eyebrows turned up, she wore a beautiful tweed suit with high heels shoes.

On knocking the door, a voice said, "Come in."

She walked in.

"Hi, I'm Mrs Holland; you called me?"

"Yes, I did, so you're the ex-wife, are you?"

"Why? Is there another?"

"Not that I know of."

"Any children, have you?"

"Not by me, he hasn't."

"What did you mean by that?"

"Well, he's had affairs with other women, and some of them could have had children by him."

"Who's this?"

"Roger Jefferson. He was going to meet at Paddington train station on the day he 'was killed,"

"I've no idea who he or she was. It couldn't be something to do with the case, and he'd worked on."

"Was it the one he was working on for Mrs England?"

"Where is she now? She's Not in the phone book I've looked through it."

"I don't know where she is or who she is."

"The DNA test proved that Benny was the father of her son."

"Was he?"

"Tell me, Jackie, have you ever heard him speak of this boy?"

"No, I never heard him say he had a son. He never told me."

"He had a brother named Terry."

"What happened to him?"

"Terry, he went to live in London somewhere, but where I've no idea."

"I've no doubt she may know' we must find her and speak to her or if you prefer."

"I will speak to my boss in the morning when she comes in."

"Are you sure you wouldn't like to speak to her yourself?"

"Whatever you think is the best doctor."

"That's not good enough. Someone killed your ex-husband, and you show as if you don't care. Why were you divorced?"

"Because he had affairs and 'he was always working. He was never home."

She left the hospital, returned to her office. Later that day, Sgt Marriott arrived on the scene, with the pathologist Doctor Angela Christie.

A middle-aged white woman with auburn hair, wearing a pair of contact lenses, the doctor lived alone with just a dog called Sid.

They placed the bagged body into their van, and it was taken to the undertakers by two morticians.

She examined the body of the girl and found a red mark on her bare backside where she had 'been' smacked, and cuts and bruises when she went through the glass window, "Did she fall or was she pushed?"

That night, Marriott started to investigate as he entered a white building, looking at the Number 7 Gospel Street. Entering the premises, he turned and saw it.

He took out a nail file from the top pocket of his jacket, placed it into the lock and forced open the door. With a torch, he looked around the room; there, on the desk, he found a file with the names Maxwell and Jennings.

"Did they know each other?"

Seating himself at the desk, he started to read it. From outside, he heard a noise, and as he turned around, he saw a woman standing over him, she pointed a silver pearl-handled pistol at his head.

"Don't move, Mr!" He placed his hands on the desk with a finger and thumb. He removed his warrant card.

"DS Marriott, madam. Who are you, madam?"

"I'm his ex-wife, Jackie Mary Holland. I've just come from the hospital; he's dead."

"Is he?"

After leaving the premises, he entered his car, putting the key into the ignition. He started it up when the wheels came loose, and the vehicle crashed into a tree, killing him instantly.

Lisa parsons were on her way home when she found his body. She entered the phone box, picked up the receiver and rang the police. The phone rang for several minutes.

While waiting, she scanned through the headlines of the Delay Star that had ''been left there… Inside the newspapers, she found a postcard. She turned it over and read it, **"To Benny, I need your help, signed E."**

She was about to put the card into her handbag when a voice said, "Just a moment, I'm putting you to through to the desk stagnate."

She was about to say, "Get a move on, I don't have all day. Where are they?" when a man voice spoke, "Hello, can I help you?"

"Yes, you can; it's about time too."

"What's this about, madam?"

"Murders…"

"Whose?"

"Mr Holland's and a police officer."

"They're dead, are they?"

"Yes, they are, I'm waiting for an answer… Are you are going to investigate those deaths, are you?"

"Stay where you are; the madam, DCI Victoria Campbell, and DS Glen Rogers, two of my CID officers are on their way. Thank you, madam, that will be all."

'She put down the phone. She stood outside the phone box and waited. It was cold.

She was a beautiful woman, wearing a grey suit with a pair of high heel shoes. She had the '**Grace Kelly**' look about her.

She didn't waste any time explaining to them. Her face ''was wrinkled like an apricot; her hair was the colour of the snow that's on the ground.

She stood up, clutched an Iceland – carrier bag. At around ten o'clock that Saturday morning, Chief Inspector Campbell and Detective Sergeant Rogers arrived at the scene. They spoke to her, "What's going on, madam?"

"Murder," she announced.

"Yes, you said when you rang the station. Where are the bodies?"

They're in burling over the road. ''They were just about to cross the street to examine ''them when the bodies were carried out by two paramedics into an ambulance.

"Where are you taking those bodies?" the Inspector, asked to the hospital mortuary, "Could you please wait? I want to look at Benny's body" She looked at the body and said, "I'm satisfied that the body is his, you've got the wrong man?"

When they arrived at the mortuary, a female pathologist, Maxine Fisher, a middle-aged white woman with black hair, dressed in a pair of overalls, exuded the bodies of both the girl and that of a mystery man.

Her verdict was that they 'were murdered. A witness had been found and confessed that a friend of his was involved in those killings and that the mafia had ordered that, but there

20

was no proof that they were behind those deaths, on the night of those murders.

A short Jamaican male had seen leaving the Brendan Theatre. Witnesses said they saw a man getting into a dark blue car that looked a lot like Benny Holland's.

The witnesses jotted down the number of the car that they claimed had driven away. He's charges face on the day of his funeral; a stranger turned up' he looks like Mr Holland.

The funeral service took place at Benson Chemainmon on Wednesday, May 30 at 11.00 am. In Ashmore chapel with family and friends, there were a lot of floral tributes but whose funeral was it?

Benny's ex couldn't keep her eyes off this person, was he her ex-husband? The body was buried in the memorial garden in a marked grave, with the words:

Those we love don't go away. They live within us every day.

Who's he? She asked herself. *He's a dead ringer for Benny. Could he have faked his death to get away from the mafia? Who was the elderly gent in the black suit that stood beside the graves?*

She was convinced this man was her ex. She couldn't believe her eyes when she saw the man's face. Was he Benny or not?

Finney's Family Tree

His great-grandfather was Tommy Wilde,
　　In the summer of 1903;
　　He married housewife, Sandy Jones.
　　His job was a tram driver.
　　Her mother was Jenny Alexander.
　　In 1913, she married Major Simon Doyle
　　An army officer.
　　He was born in 1802.
　　She was born in 1806, her job,
　　'Was a hospital librarian.
　　He'd married a woman young enough,
　　To be his daughter, so people said.
　　All other members of the girl's family went off to fight in
the war,
　　'And were killed on the Somme in 1916.
　　They only had two children: Frank born in 1915, and Cilia
1917;
　　Their youngish Cilia kept a diary. 'This helps her to cope,
　　With a life of being cut off from her friends in the outside
world.
　　When they were thirteen, they went into hiding,
　　From the Germans, with six other people.
　　She grew up. In 1937, she Married Michael John Finney,
　　A medical forensic investigator.
　　Six years later, their only son, Patrick,
　　Was born in a Council house in London on the 17
February 1942 ;
　　His school was in London.
　　His job was an RAF Officer.
　　And lead his team that took part in

The Battle of Britain.

Cilia's diary: Today is Wednesday: a nice one.

Father went off to fight in WW2.

Mother started home and looked after the
Younger ones.

I'll move out and take Johnny.

The diary with me and someday, I'll have children,
Of my own and I hope they'll never have to go through,
What I did. My brother, Frank, flowed father and joined
up.

Today, I got the terrible news about Frank,
Killed! The war took him too.

Mother just sat in the old black rocking chair under the
window, rereading father's letter. 'She'd' read it' 'over' 'and
over again 'when this is all over, I will find myself a boyfriend
with money and buy a big house."

The Case of the Missing Lion

Finney started investigating the footprints in the hallway at May Field Hall and found another body of a woman with the look of the devil on her face. As if she was running away from someone when she fell dead.

She 'was located with her throat slit from both sides.

At around ten o'clock, he arrived at Mayfield Hall, queried the staff and asked where they were on the day of inquisition.

"Where were you on the day the murder took place, did you see anything like a big black lion cat or something like that?"

"No, sir, I was here all day at the Hall dusting the corners off the desk and didn't see anything like that, sir, just a man in old clothes sitting on the well, that had been left outside the other day, by the madam. Why do you want to know, sir?"

"I like to know who the man was in the red overcoat and why was he running away when he saw the police officers come towards him?

"Last week, someone was killed, up at the big house in Craddock Manner. We're looking for anyone who may have seen a big black lion cat that escaped from the zoo some weeks ago.

"Who was that tall man that walked out through the cast iron gate on the day of Mrs June Lesson's death? Do you know who he was?"

"I've no idea, sir. I've only started working here a week ago.

"I wouldn't know. They're not my kind of people, sir.

"Someone heard a scream and came running out of the shop shouting, 'ha you, stop!', but the person ran off."

"Who was he and what was he doing there on that day? Do you know him at all?

"Does he work there?"

"No, he doesn't sir. I've never seen him before, until that day. A week ago, he came back to see our cook, Mrs VERA Rock More."

"What did he want with her?

"Could I speak to her?"

"She's off today, sir, she doesn't work on Tuesdays. He said he'd come about grader's job he'd seen advertised in our window, the day before."

"Then what?"

"He just got up and left, and three days later, his body was discovered in the woods by Martin Hauxwell, a walker, who found a pair of his old brown boots. Were they his? Do you know?"

"No, they belong to Sir John Mayfield. They went missing two weeks ago, sir."

"Is there a Mrs Mayfield, do you know?"

"There was."

"What happened to her?"

"She left, so I 'was told."

"Any idea where she is now?"

"The last I heard, she was in London, but that was a year ago sir, she was working for a doctor, Dr Colin Perry Rendell."

"Where can we find him, is he in the phone book, what part of London does he live in?"

"I wouldn't know... I'm not from London myself, sir. I'm just working class."

"What's your job?"

"I do the washing and wash up the silver knives and forks."

"Where do you do that?"

"In the kitchen sink. The Mayfields consider ''them to be upper-class people, they're a law unto themselves they are, and they've never done a day's work in their line."

"What about Dr Rendell? Is he the upper class too?"

"No, he's not, he's just working class like myself, and he's one of us – a good guy."

"When did you last see him?"

"It was the day the bodies were found or was it afterwards?"

"No, it was the day he came to Mayfield Hall to speak to Sir John."

"What did he want with him, was it to do with the heart attack that he had two years ago, or was it about the missing money, was it?"

"No, it was about his brother Hugh's letter he received four weeks ago from him with notes cut of a newspaper warning him to stay away from the hall."

"Why?"

"They were written with a pen. One of ''his' boots went missing from 'his' hotel bedroom where; he stayed."

"Do you know who sent these notes to him, do you?"

"I think they couldn't come from his friend Sir Charles Bake."

"Who's he and when he's at home?"

"He was in the army with Sir John when he stayed in South America some years ago."

"What happened to him, did he die in the war?"

"No, he's alive and living with his family. On the big estate just over the green, sir."

"What does he look like?"

"He's a tall, bearded man with glasses and smokes a pipe, but the other day, I saw a man in a brown overcoat following him in a black cab. A police officer in a car was following the cab."

"Do you know who's in the police car?"

"Yes, it was Inspector Sidney Burrows."

"Did he see you at all?"

"No, he didn't, but I saw your friend, the good doctor Brian Maynard. He's staying up at the house, isn't he sir?"

"Yes, he is investigating agreement between two savant girls, Kathryn and Natasha. Do you know what the row was about?"

"Yes, it was over the young Mayfield and Money, sir."

"Why?"

"Because they've got it and we haven't They look down on people like us, and they could get away with murder; they could."

"I know my place, sir."

"Where's that?"

"It's working here, sir."

"What happened to the other girl that worked here?"

"She left because Mr Mayfield caught her, three weeks earlier, stealing money from his wall safe,"

"What did he do, did he call the police, did he at all?"

"No, he didn't, he dealt with her himself."

"What was her name?"

"Fiona Carmichael, sir."

"Ms or Mrs?"

"Ms Carmichael, sir. She was a lovely girl, so, we all thought."

"Did she walk a stick or not?"

"No, she was in a wheelchair. She was born with spinal meningitis, but when she came to work here, our head housekeeper, Mrs Appellation, was mistaken for Mrs Mayfield, sir."

"Was she now, why was that do you think?"

"I've no idea, sir, some say they looked like sisters, others say they are."

"Were they?"

"No, they weren't."

"Who was the face at the window?"

"I've no idea who the face at the window was."

The trail led Finney to a rundown two room's shack in the woods at the back of the hall.

Finney walked down the stairs and pushed open the door of the cabin where he found a set of footprints leading to the end of the entrance to the kitchen and on the floor. He found blood-stained clothing that was belonging to Mrs Mayfield, or did they? He asked,

"How tall was she?"

"About five-eight."

"Eyes?"

"Dark blue."

He followed the trail to an open door through the garden. There, he found the body of a young woman with her throat cut.

He didn't believe for a minute that the woman wouldn't go there alone on a night to meet with this mystery, man, whoever he was. He could almost hear himself say, *murder*.

When he stopped by the door and found bloodstains on the carpet near the outside door, he caught Colonel Goodwin in an empty room with a candle. He asked what he was doing in there, but 'he left the room and refused to answer his questions about what 'he was doing in there and who was he signalling 'to.

Was it their son Sinned, who had come back to seek revenge for his family estate and claimed that it was stolen from them, his uncles lost it in a card game or did he...?

No, he had sold the estate because the family had fallen into such hard times that 'the eldest son dropped out of school and ended up working, sweeping nightclub floors for a living to help the family.

"Was this the body of Mrs Mayfield?" he asked himself, "What was it that the girl says that Mrs Mayfield went to work in London for the doctor, but who was he and where was he now? Because he wasn't in the phone book."

"' The post-mortem placed the time of death at around two in the afternoon and the police evidence retted on the winces statement only, and why did the police drop the case, did they know something that no-one else knew, like the name of the killer?"

Mayfield hall lay between Bilston and Waynesfield Canal. At about 6 p.m. on that day, the body of Mr Clive Blackrock was found at the bottom of the cut on Tuesday the 22nd of July, 1960. His collection ''was never found and the case 'was closed

The Mayfield family supposed a course since the youngest of the family had sold his soul to the devil. That's when it all started.

A few days later, Doctor Colin Rendell arrived from London. He took a taxi to the museum when he met his old friend, Jake George Basher.

It was five to six when the taxi got to the museum. The driver stopped outside the mime door. He reached out and walked up to the steps and in through the big glass doors when finally they met each other.

The good doctor spoke, "It's good to see you after all those years, what you been up to?"

"What do you mean by that remark?" he asked him.

"Nothing, just that I'm glad to see you again. I thought that you were dead, so I was told."

"No, I'm not. I've been away working on a case."

"What case?"

"The case of the businessman Paul Street, who was found dead on his yacht in Switzerland some years ago; he 'was beaten around his head with the blunt instrument."

"Any idea who did this?"

"The Police have Della Phillipa Mason in for it; she's the woman who lived with him on the yacht at the time."

"Where is yacht now?"

"It's in dry dock. ''She's my client."

A few minutes later, his phone rang. 'He took it out of his jacket pocket, opened it up and spoke: "Hello, who's this?"

"It's Ms Della Mary Jackson here."

"Oh; hello', 'what can 'I do for you', 'madam......?"

"Tell me more about how much she's willing to pay, to get out of this?"

"Why, what's it got to you?"

"She was with me at the time he 'was killed. We were having dinner in a pub called The Two Herds Are Better Than One, until two."

"She's paying me five hundred pounds a day to find the truck driver, who she said, saw her transporting at the time so..." he said.

"Did she get the license number of that truck? It's the key to the whole case. Tell her not to sign anything or make any statement until I see her later on today."

Ms Jackson put her phone into her handbag and walked into the room. She slowly walked around the desk and slid into the armchair next to Ms Mason.

They just sat there with their arms around each other, as if they were schoolgirls rather than women. She cried on her shoulder and admitted the night before he 'was killed that they were lovers and they'd make love.

The Inspector spoke understandable English and turned to them and asked what they were up to, "What are you doing?" he asked.

Ms Mason pushed her straight back and stopped.

"I didn't kill him, and I'll not say any more than that, Inspector, until my lawyer gets here."

"Come on, Ms Masson, tell me where you were going after you left the Luxury pub?"

"He couldn't have taken the yacht out that night, Inspector."

"Why not?"

"Because there was high tide. What was 'he' did, taking the yacht out at sea on that rainy night like that? Any idea Inspector, what he was doing there?"

"No idea, you tell me? His body 'was' found on the starboard side, and besides, on the floor of the upper deck, we found a bloody imprint of a woman's shoe, is it your, madam?"

"No, I don't wear those kinds of shoes. 'I wouldn't be seen dead in those shoes, Inspector."

"Why, what's wrong with them?"

"They're too cheap and downmarket for me. You want to drag others into this murder case too?"

"No, I don't. I'm afraid I'm not at liberty to tell you that, madam."

'He pushed his chair back, got up to his feet and walked over to the window of his office, looked out through it and saw a woman in a red coat, hat and light brown high heel shoes. She was on her phone, but who was she calling?

"It couldn't be me. My phone hasn't rung all day, and it has to be that Private Detective Finney, he's up at Mayfield Hall, investigating. That will keep him out of my air for a while, but what of his friend the excellent doctor, Maynard the ex-marine, where is he?"

The Times newspaper lay on his desk, and he read the letter page telling him about the case. Someone had put a letter in the paper asking if anyone who had seen the killing, to come forward and to offer a reward to anyone, who may have seen the killer.

He leaned back in his chair thinking about this doctor fellow that lived in London, who were the flowers from, found with an empty wine bottle on the floor of her bedroom and a notice addressed to Finney signed, Tammy Nelson.

"Who's she, where can I find her, is she the killer?"

"The victim was found bare-footed, but why did the killer take off their shoes? Was it so that no one would hear him or her?"

"It's a strange case; many questions need to be asked, like why wasn't anyone listening when asked these questions, and they were all afraid to answer his questions. Why was this? Had someone get to them or paid them not to say anything?"

"Did Mr Finney ask them when he spoke to the staff at Mayfield Hall? Did he? I don't think he did, someone has blood on their hands, and we need to find them before they kill again."

"What of the big black lion cat, where it is now and who does the dander belong 'to….? Why wasn't it found, did the killer take it with them and why did they cover the body with a Union Jack flag, what is it the killer is trying to tell us?"

"Someone knows something, and they do not tell us."

"Why is this?"

It was later that Friday when Jacob Reinhard Pulaski, her lawyer, emerged the police station. He walked up to the stairs and pushed the door open of a private room and smiled, as the girl who sat behind the desk, asked, "Good morning, sir. How can I help you?"

"Yes, I'm looking for Ms Mason. 'Can you tell me where I can find her place?"

"She's in a cell just on your left, and she's got someone with her, sir."

"Who Ms Mason, love?"

"Who are you, sir? And I'm not your love sir!?" she said

"I'm her lawyer."

"Are you? She already has someone with her, sir."

"Yes, I noticed that officer."

"They've been waiting for you."

"They, who're they?"

"The young Mayfield."

"Well, I'm here now," as he walked into the room, he opened the door, and the officer handed him a written statement, "Whose is this?"

He walked along the corridor and past the inspector office.

Pulaski opened the door, popped his head around it and said to the female officer that sat outside the door

"I'm here to see," he asked.

, "MS Mason's …" sir? She was told not to do this, wasn't she?"

She laughed and said, "You can't win, sir!"

He said, "There's something crooked about this murder at Mayfield Hall, isn't there?"

His phone rang; he answered it, "Yes… 'this is Mr Pulaski…just a moment." He placed his hand over the mouthpiece.

Murder She Stuttered

On a late September day in 1996, Sidney Charles Perks arrived at Kensington College and went into the gents for a crafty smoke.

He sneaked behind the cubical and removed a contained cigarette from a white, small, square box and took one out. 'Placed the smoke in his mouth.

He was about to light it when he heard noise creeping behind him! A male person, named Arthur Barrington Watson sneaked out of the cubical two, grabbed Perks from behind with a tie that he placed around his neck and choked the life out of him. He felt the cold kiss of death flicker across his throat!

The killer escaped through a hole in the roof. He jumped down to the floor and walked across the road into a waiting car.

The driver of the red car drove away with him in it. No one had missed Perks all day. They all thought that he'd gone home, sick like he always did.

It wasn't until 3:30 pm early that afternoon, when Polly Craddock, the cleaning lady, arrived at the college, the West Indian woman in her late fourths, the too early fifties, plump as she stood about four foot ten with glasses.

She started mopping around the floor and was cleaning washbasins as she turned her head slowly and noticed the door of cubic one was jammed shut. In her Jamaican voice, she said, "Is there anyone in there? Come on, man, come out of there."

She's an exciting person who liked to know what was going on. As she got to the door of the cubical one, with her right foot, she pushed open the door. There on the floor, a male body was lying facing downwards in the gents toilets.

"All right, sir?" she asked, but there was no response.

She dropped the mop on the floor, reached out and ran to the security desk, stuttering her heard off.

"Murder!" she shouted out at the top of her voice. The security officer, Tax Corey, was a tall Jamaican male in his sixties, built like Tyson.

He asked, "What's the matter, Polly? You look as if you've just seen a ghost, have you?"

"Murder," she mumbled.

"Murder? 'Who's been murdered?" asked Tex.

He walked up to her and asked, "Where?"

"There's a body in the gents. This way, sir. Follow me," they entered the toilet.

"Which one?"

Polly spoke, "the body in cubical one!"

Tax walked over to cubical one where the body was 'He looked in the cubical. There he found the person's body, face down.

"your right, Polly. What's the matter with him? Is he asleep? What time did you find the body?"

"Just after I came on about 3.40, give or take an hour sir."

Like Tex's on his face when he turned the body over and felt the praise, but there was nothing.

"Is he alright?"

"No, he's dead."

"Is he? Who's done it?"

"I don't know who's done it. It's not my job; that's for the police to find out."

"That's the missing student 'Perks'. We've been looking for him for hours. He went absent from his class an hour ago and told us that he wasn't well. We all thought that he'd gone home when he hadn't."

They left the body there and walked to the office, called the Wellington Road Police Station when they heard the shot came through the classroom window. It shattered the glass to bits.

"We'd better phoned the police, hadn't we?"

Walking back to his office, he picked up the phone and dialled 999 to get through to the telephone exchange on the switchboard. A pretty voice spoke, "Can I help? Which service do you require, sir?"

"Police...we've found a body. It's one of our old students. He has been' murdered."

She muttered, "Calm down, sir. I'll put you through to WPC Deraa Reno. A 22-years-old black female asked where and what time did this happen?"

"We've found the victim at college in the gents at about 3.40, this afternoon!"

"Hold on. I'll put you through to the CID office." The phone rang in the empty office.

"There's no one in there, sir."

She put the phone down. In the background, the sound of opera music played, but where; was it, coming 'from....?

Later that afternoon just after five, Detective Inspector Emma Secombe arrived at the office. She caught Detective Sergeant Milligan, sitting at the desk with his foot up, with a pair of headphones on his head.

He was listening to his opera music, "That bloody opera", she heard herself say, as she walked to the door, turned the handle, walked out down the stairs and into the office.

She walked over to her desk, "Nothing to do Milligan. Didn't you hear the phone ringing?"

"Nah, it's all quiet ma'am; everyone's behaving. What about you?"

"Come on here. Turn that music off. We've got a student murder to solve."

"What? Is the college murdering their students, are they? I've heard they were thrown out but never been murdered."

"They have now found a body in the gents, and the supper wants to see us."

"What about?"

"The murder. What do you think ''he wanted? About not your music."

Leaving the office, they took a short walk down a corridor, crossed the hallway, up to 'two flights of stairs and came to a light-coloured door with a shola window, with a sign saying *Chief Super Tenant Rivers*; an older man with glasses sat behind a desk.

In his lifetime, he'd faced a lot of challenges; lost his brother and his only son, and his wife had left him some years ago for another man who'd killed her. He'd worked on the case but never found the one who did it.

The Inspector knocked on the door. A voice said, "Come in." She turned the handle, opened the door and walked in. She stood there as if she was going to 'be' told off for not doing her homework; as if she was back at school.

"Yes, sir, you wanted to see me, sir;"

"Yes, Inspector, there's been a murder at old college. Back then, it was called Greenwood."

"It's now called Kensington, sir, built-in 1720, was it, sir?"

"Wrong, Inspector! It 'was built in 1820, my girl." In my school, you would 'be' spanked for that. It's my way or the high way, Inspector and does as you 'are told unless you want a spanking. Do you?"

"No, I don't like anyone to touch my backside."

"Well, we better find this killer before he kills again." When the door opened, in walked Detective Sergeant Ernie John Milligan.

"Milligan, are you related to Spike, are you?"

"No, I'm not related to him."

They were about to leave the Super office when he turned and pointed at Detective Sergeant Milligan.

"I want a word with you."

"What's up and what's he been up to, sir?"

"He's been buying stolen goods from Vincent Wildman, in a pub called the Crown and Skins."

"What stolen goods?"

"CDs and DVDs from Kirk's record's shop."

"Oh, yes! Mixing with those kinds of folks, are you?"

"He's a mate."

"He's a crook Milligan, and you could go down for this."

He leaned forward to her and said, "I have no idea what you are on about, and I didn't know they 'were nicked."

"Oh, didn't you?"

"Why didn't he tell you? I thought he was your mate?"

"Yes, he is my mate."

"Did you know a shop was broken into, two or three days ago and the owner, Thomas Eugene Kirk, a fifty-five-year-old man was found dead?"

"Oh!"

"I give you shoot! Were you in on it with him, were you!?"

What, me?"

"Yes, you!"

"Not me, sir. I'm a police officer, not a murderer."

"Not for long, you won't be if you didn't tell me how you came by those things."

"I'm a victim of fraud, sir. My ID has stolen some works."

"You haven't reported it yet, have you?"

"I haven't had time to, sir. I was caught up in a high-speed car chase. It happened on the motorway!

"I was trying to get away from a violent man driving like a madman, sir, who knocked me off the road. It wasn't for a traffic cop James Potter. 'I wouldn't be here to speak to you now, sir. Thanks to the boys in blue, I got away safely, sir."

They left the office and walked down the stairs out through the door to a car.

Where detective Constable Yonne Seller sat, "Oh, no, it's the guvnor," she moaned. 'They got into a blue car and drove to the scene. Milligan cried, "We're like the three musketeers, aren't we? One for all and all for one."

"Ya and none you Milligan,"

Yonne put an Elvis Presley CD on the CD player: *Jailhouse Rock*. Milligan moaned, "Oh, no! Not rock n' roll. I can't stand the bloody thing."

Yonne spoke, "It's better than your opera, isn't it?"

They arrived on the scene, and the inspector nodded to a female pathologist, Maxine Fisher: a middle-aged female with black hair, dressed in a pair of white overalls that exuded the body.

"Well, doctor," Maxine spoke, "an IC one male has been strangled and choked to death Inspector." she turned to Sergeant Milligan, who sat in the back of the car and took off his flat black shoes.

"Why have you taken your shoes off, sergeant?"

"That's a funny question, isn't it, ma'am? Why people take off their shoes?"

"When their feet hurt or if they go padding in the sea when they watch the telly, with their feet up, sitting on a sofa after a hard day's work."

"What work? You have not done a thing but sit in the car with your shoes off. What do you think; this is a seaside place?"

He put his shoes back on and walked over to her, "What that got to do with the case, ma'am?"

"I was asking you. Now let's get on with the case, will you, and find this killer."

"Who was the last person to see him alive, ma'am?"

"The one that killed him; that's Seconders' law."

"Is it, we don't know who he is, ma'am?"

"Then go and find out who he or she could be?"

"A good detective will keep asking who, when and why to go and interview the students, will you? We don't have all day."

They interviewed an ex-student, Frank Reeves; a 33-year-old male sat there in the interviews room, they entered the room and switched on a tape.

"Time is 1.57 p.m. Friday, 15th August 1996. Well, Mr Reeves, can you tell us about the disputes between you and the victim and what happened?"

"One was about him standing a good friend's name All over the college."

"Didn't you say that you'd kill him?"

"Yes, but I didn't mean murder."

"Then what did you mean?"

"I meant that I'd call my friend and tell him what he said behind his back."

"You're telling us that you never liked him."

"No, I didn't. I hated ''his guts."

"Why?"

"He's a mean, selfish, tight-fisted, unfeeling person who only thought about himself."

"You don't kill people because they won't spend money and on the day in question, a female tutor threw you out of her class, didn't she, sir? Why was that? Can you tell us!?"

"Yes, because she'd sided with him."

"What did you say to her? Was that 'I'd spank you'? Didn't you say that, sir?"

"Yes, she needs it."

"Does she Now, why is that? Going to take her over your knee, were you, sir?"

"Yes, I was until someone stopped him…"

"Who?"

"It was Mr Watson."

"How many students were in the class?"

"About five or six," he said as she took him back to a cell to think about it. Their next interview took place in the classroom with Leticia Warner: a 31-year-old female university lecturer, with long dark brown hair that came down to her back. She's dressed more like a man, than a woman, in jeans and polo-necked sweater.

'When was the last time you saw Mr Perks?"

"I've not seen him for a week, Inspector, and he's not attended this class since the disputes with Mr Reeves."

"Did they have descended often?"

"About three or four times a week. I had to tell Mr Reeves about his conduct, and he 'was suspended twice; a bit of a complainer and an interior, who shoves his nose into other people's affairs when he 'is told to keep it out, and if anyone upsets his friends, he goes off and does his avenging angel act. Many times, I threw him out of my class because he'd harassed me on the phone and he'd threatened Mr Perks that he's sent some lads around to his flat to rub him out!"

"Kill him, you mean?"

"Yes."

"Did he say that he was going to put you over his knee and spank you?"

"Yes, he did."

"How far did he get?"

"He just slipped me on the backside, when I bent over the desk."

"Where is he? His name doesn't seem to be on the register."

"No, it's not, Inspector."

"Where does he live?"

She handed the Inspector his address, "He lives at Fury Thee Fallyfoot way."

"Thank you."

Milligan was chatting to his old friends when the Inspector walked over to him and said "Oi! Come on here."

"Ardon, we are supposed to be finding Mr Perks' killer."

"Why to bother; everyone I spoke to said nobody liked him!"

"Did they now; can we find him here?"

"It could be that Sid Miler."

"He haired up the college because they threw him out. He wrote fifteen litters to the principal about it, and he was too to stay away from there."

"How do you know it's him, ma'am?"

"It could be a woman named Sid?"

"We don't know how to get on to HQ and find out if he is a she."

"Well, we won't find him with you were standing there, chatting with your old friends will we."

"Never mind that. We still have to find ''his killer."

"Someone wanted revenge; didn't he? What of the hit list we've found the names 'on. It is Gordon Roberts, Michael Martin and Milligan's name on there."

You're on the list; what have you done to him!"

"Nothing."

"Then why is your name on his hit list, can you tell me?"

"I've no idea, ma'am."

"Go back to Mr Reeves's flat and bring him back in."

"Why?"

"Do it, will you? He was not a nice man. A year ago, he stabbed a police officer outside a train station at Fort William, in Scotland and got away with it!"

"Mum…ma'am."

"What do you mean Mum… What's all that about?"

"You silly man, get out of my office, heaven's sake, just do as I say."

He drove to the address, and as he sat in the car, his brain tried to work out what was going on. He arrived at Mr Glen Reeves's flat and rang the intercom. Glen picked it up and spoke, "Yes, who are you, and what do you want?"

"Police, sir. Detective Sergeant Milligan. May I come in, please?"

"What is it?"

"I'd rather come inside, Mr Reeves if you don't mind. We can't talk out here, sir, everyone will know about it, won't they?"

"Alright, come in."

"What's it about, officer?"

"The stabbing of DC Mason in Scotland, a year ago, sir."

"What about it?"

"Weren't you the one who did it?"

"No, it won't surprise me."

"You were there on the day, and you 'were seen running away, weren't you, sir?"

"Yes, but I'm not the one who did it."

"What about the body found in the gents at college. Did you kill Mr Perks? My governor said it was you."

"She's a liar, and she needs a spanking."

"I 'wouldn't say that if I were you, sir."

"Why not?"

"What was that sir, you just said? Let's get back to the question. 'Where were you on the night in question?"

"I was home all day, and I didn't get out of bed until after ten, officer."

"Did you go out at all, sir?"

"No, it rained all day, so I stayed in."

"Was there anyone with you, and what of the rape of WPC Monroe and you with your trousers down? What was going on, sir?"

"She likes sex games, where she spanked me."

"So that's why the charges were dropped because you were going to tell on her, weren't you, sir?"

"Yes, I was."

That morning, a copy of the Times newspaper came through his door; the clock on his wall started ticking so loud that he could hear it above the noise of the rain outside that smashed against his window.

"Sorry, sir, I've got to take your income."

As they were leaving, Milligan turned his head, looked over to the desk, "You like reading, do you?"

He nodded, "Sometimes I read a book with the music playing in the background on the CD player. I enjoy both of those unless I'm out with a woman having a candle-lit dinner for two. Why do you want to know this?"

"I wonder why WPC Monroe didn't bring you in, and if it gets out that a female officer was doing that kind of thing to men, she could lose her job. I'll show you a photograph of you and her, playing sex games. Is this you, sir?"

"How did you get that!?"

"It was found at the scene... Can you tell me how it got there, sir?"

"Someone could've put it there, officer!"

"Like who?"

"The killer."

"What would the killer want with a photograph of you unless he was blackmailing?"

"You was he, sir? Come on; I'm you taking in."

"I have a gun in my pocket. You move, and you're dead!" 'he shook his head.

42

Murder in the Shadows

It was 2.50 a.m. by the station clock, on a snowy Monday morning, in the of the middle of winter. The moon gleamed through the station window, icy roads and snowstorms.

PC Tyler had arrived at Bridgewater HQ for his graveyard shift. It was his first day of duty, and he 'was sent out on the streets.

PC Tyler and WPC Frances Mary Garland, while on their beat in Benso, found a body in an upstairs bedroom, on the bed, when they broke the door down of the Gold Pen house on a breezy Sunday morning in May 2007.

That day, they received several phone calls from a nosey neighbour who claimed she hadn't seen Mrs Gold Pen for some weeks and thought that he'd killed her.

Mrs Higgins was a small woman, between 70 and 75 years old, who'd pestered the police, told the officers that they were always arguing constantly in public streets, pubs and shopping centres.

Charles, a small-time crook, was suspected of murdering his wife, who was found naked on her bed, with her hands and feet bound, bludgeoned to death.

"I saw him leave their home in a hurry at around 6.30 that morning, officers."

"Where' was he going at that time of the morning? Does he work, madam?"

"I'm not sure, officer. I've never heard anyone say he'd worked for a living."

In the early hours on the day of her murder, Charles had left their home. At the scene, on the floor, lying beside her body, they found the murder weapon: an ice pick that 'was covered in blood.

Tara Vanessa Slater was born In the East end of London on the 8th of January. 1981. She was of mixed parentage and, 'was educated at Thornton's Girls High School.

She's an ordinary girl from a wealthy family who grew up in an industrial town. They were upper-class people that came from the other side of the street.

Ten years ago, Tyler met Tara at a college open day, when she was a contestant in a beauty pageant and was crowned the college queen for the second year running.

'She was nicknamed 'Buttercup' because she wore buttercups in her hair. He was just a cadet, aged 21, just finding his feet. She was an 18-year-old college student; studied English and drama.

Her mother, Natasha Wong, born on 13th October 1925 in Singapore, was nicknamed the Iron Lad. 'She' ruled with a rod of iron, a Thatcher look-alike. Tara's father was born on July 3rd, 1923, in Honolulu, the capital of Hawaii.

Natasha met Jack Slater – nicknamed Jocko – in 1956, when she worked as a receptionist in a hospital, in Singapore, while he worked for the Hong Kong Police Force, this was his first job before he became an MP. They'd moved to England and got married at Westminster Abbey.

In the same year, England won the World Cup, beating West Germany four-two. It was quite a fair with just a few of their closest friends.

She wanted her daughter to be a film actress and marry a famous actor like Robert Wagner, Redford, but the dream never happened.

On a frosty Tuesday morning, in mid-February, Constable Tyler walked through the same bus station where the murder took the place of a 25-year-old college dropout.

Her lifeless body was found on a bus station bench earlier that day before 9.50. Constable Tyler walked through the station after his late-night shift to catch the 526 bus home.

Constable Tyler stumbled across a body while walking through Westhampton Bus Terminal, to catch a bus at the same time as the murder.

He turned his head and looked around and heard a sound of someone breaking glass, he shouted, "Hey, who's that!" but there was no one there.

Tyler approached the victim, noticed a figure – dirty, dressed in rags as if she had come from the poorhouse, lying there wasn't breathing.

He thought the person was just asleep, but when he approached the figure and saw who it was and when he turned the body over, he stared at the person's face and tried to revive her.

"Oh, no, it can't be her. 'Not my girl Tara. Those bastards have killed her! What will Lord Slater say when he hears about his girl 'being' murdered….?"

Tyler couldn't adjust himself knowing that she's dead now and he'd never see this girl alive again.

He cried, "I loved you. Why did you leave me for him?" Buttercup, a politician's daughter, who disappeared in the early days of February 2006, was found sleeping rough on the street.

She was a bit of a drama queen when it came to love. She'd go off and tell all people what man did to her in her bedroom and the sex games they'd played.

She ended up begging on the streets. She asked, stole and borrowed. Tyler took a nip of Spring Water and thought to himself; *He'll blame me like he always did. He never likes him one bit. He always felt that she was too good for the likes of me.* She'd been thrown out of the family home after an argument with her father.

That weekend, her father came home early and pushed the open door of his private studies. He'd walked in on her and caught her stealing money from his wall safe.

"What you think you're doing!"

"I need the money, father."

"It's not money that you need, my girl! It's a good spanking you should have had years ago."

"Come then, father, put me across your knee," her eyes looked at him standing there, waiting for him to do what he said he'd do, but he did nothing.

She pulled up her shirt, "Are you going to do it? Come on, take my panties down and spank my backside like you always did when I was a kid."

"I couldn't sit down for weeks; my backside was red all over through you. 'The kids in my class looked at me. I had to sit on a cushion for weeks."

She pulled down her panties and bent over his desk and said, "Come on, father. What you are waiting for?"

"You wouldn't like it if I did."

He slapped her on her backside and spoke to her, "get up and get out."

She pulled her panties up, left through the door and said to him, "You like to spank women, don't you, father? I'm making my point, Father. Why should that matter to you?"

"Go… Will you? You talk too much."

He walked her to the door, opened it, and threw her out of the house. She pulled her panties up and her skirt down to her knees; smacked herself on the backside.

She walked down the stairs, crossed to the hallway, out the door, and she said to herself, "That hurt!"

"That's what I need, a good smack, isn't it father? And a good man to put me over his knee. Can you find me one? Because they're only after one thing from me is sex and foreplay. That's all they what from me."

She walked out the door and said, "Goodbye, Mr Spank. Each time, I am looking at my backside, I'll think of you!"

A week later, she was caught on college premises by a female tutor, with her panties down, shacking and having sex with male students, showing her backside for all to see. The tutor said, "What do you think you're doing? Get those panties up now!"

She 'was thrown out of college for dropping her panties on college grounds. They were going to get the police.

She was about to walk out the gate when she gave them the fourth finger in the air up yours, a miss.

The tutor, Miss Mortimer, a 55-year-old spinster, said to her, "You need your backside smacking, my girl. I'd put you across my knee if I could get away with it, and you wouldn't sit down for the next six weeks."

As she walked away, she spoke

"Any time, Miss, I won't tell anyone!"

"Come then, over here."

She walked over to where Miss Mortimer sat. On a small brick wall outside the college, facing the window.

"Yes, Miss."

"Get over my knee!"

"Yes, miss."

She lay across Miss Mortimer's knee. She pulled her skirt up and smacked her backside with her open hand that came down hard on Tara's base.

It turned red, as she got up from Miss Mortimer's knee and pulled her miniskirt down to her backside and walked to the great and said, "That hurt Miss, but I needed it, and I deserve it, didn't I?"

"Yes, you did, didn't you? does your backside hurt?"

"Yes, it does, miss. 'I won't be able to sit down for a few weeks!"

They'd pay her for sex with them on the campus, behind the bike sheds and for propositioning male tutors, who refused to have sex with her and sent her home

An announcement came over the antennae, "A body has 'been found on one of the benches at this bus station. If anyone knows anything about the victim, would they contact Bridgewater Police and speak to the investigating officer, who is leading the investigation?"

Tyler's memories flashed back to the days of his first kiss when they stood outside his flat in Benson and kissed in the rain, as he came back to himself, he stood there for a moment, bent down and looked at her dead body lying there.

Tyler decided to take the law into his own hands and investigate the murder case himself. He crossed the road to his office, walked up to the steps through the big glass door, he walked in and sat at the desk and said to himself, "I'll find you whoever you are, mate. You won't get away with this!"

It was just after three in the afternoon when he got up from his desk and left the office, pushed the door open, walked down the stairs and out through the glass door, on to the street he walked across the road to the chip shop, brought himself a big bag of chips and a bottle of Coke, muttered to himself, "It's Friday, payday. I've got to go to the bank and get some cash to pay a bill, or the lights will 'be cut off again, and I could spend another weekend in the dark."

Tyler nicknamed her father is 'Squire Jack', who thought more of his career than he did of his family."

Tyler took off his overcoat and covered her body, then kissed her forehead. When a woman in white came out of on were and spoke to him

"What's the matter, Tyler? You look as if you've just seen a ghost."

"Oh, it's you, Tara. Aren't you dead?"

"Of course, I am."

"You mean you're a ghost?"

"Look at this."

She walked straight through a plain glass window and vanished into thin air.

Her voice echoed across the station.

"I suppose you'll have to tell daddy, but of course he'll blame you. They did it, Tyler."

"Who?" He asked

"The mob, who do you think did it. Leave it alone, or you're next to die. Bye."

"Ha, come back, I'm not done with you yet. You haven't told me who's done it."

He thought, "It wasn't them!" he thought it was a loan shark, she knew and lived with at the time of her death, that did it.

'This was his style. Nicknamed 'the Sleeper', he suffocated his victims while they slept.

Tyler was told by his superiors to leave the case alone and leave it to them because of his connection with the victim, but as usual, he ignored them, and in his own time, he carried out his inquiries.

Back in the office, he sat at the desk and read the reports and a list of suspects. He read the list of names and saw his name on the list and found the name of the 'Stones'.

A loan shark, who he thought was the killer, she owed him money. He had no proof of this, the person he thought did it, but he was their primary and only suspect for her murder.

He read on and found the name of Tara's college friend, Tasha Venus Hudson, aged about 22. Tyler read the address. She lived at fourteen Loxton-Drives, Benson.

'This was a little maisonette in a cul-de-sac, in a rundown backstreet, which was condemned by the local council due to cutbacks.

Tyler thought to himself, "That's just down the road." He left the station, crossed the road and walked along the street, looking for a white, solid wooden door with small squared windows in that, 'was boarded up.

He stopped by a red brick door, approached the door and rang the doorbell. ''She was a redheaded female with foxtail hairstyle.

She wore a low-cut vest type of shirt with denim shorts and was wearing flip-flops. She appeared from the stair door, ten feet to the other door, unlatched the chain, and peered through the gap.

"Yes, 'who are you, what do you want and who do you work for?"

He showed his warrant card through the gap, "It's Constable Tyler, madam. I'm here about the Slater murder; the one in the newspapers. Can I come in and have a word with you, please?"

"You mean the one that was on the news the other day? That's tragic. Wasn't she going to marry a copper, as she said? She always said that she was a bad girl. She liked having her backside smacked, didn't she?"

"Yes, she did, but she disappeared on that day. Did she have any other boyfriends other than me, I mean?"

"No, not that I know of."

49

"Where were you on the day she 'was murdered?"

"I was home all day."

"Were there any witnesses?"

"No, only my four-year-old son, Lionel."

"Do you know who his father he is?"

"I don't know who it is. ''He was born in a lay-by on the A5, on the backseat of a black taxi in Two Thousand and Three, why do you want to know?"

"I was asking, that's all. ; He could be the killer."

"What, Billy John Fisher? He wouldn't hurt a fly."

"Who's he?"

"Just someone I used to know."

"He's dead now, isn't he?"

"Is he? How did he die?"

"He took his own life some years ago, so ''I'm told."

"How old was he?"

"At the time of his death', he was forty-four."

She walked to the porch door, pushed it open and let him in; he reached inside his jacket pocket, handed her a photograph of the victim.

"Do you know this girl?"

"Yes, I knew her from college."

"Wasn't she thrown out for having sex with male students?"

"Yes." He handed her a photograph of a suspect.

"Do you know this man?"

She stared at the photograph of a handsome young man.

"No, who's he, I've not seen him before officer?"

"A loan shark by the name of Stones, madam."

"What did you say his name was? He's supposed to be dead, killed in a car explosion in 1970, officer. Wasn't it in all the newspapers and on the radio and TV News?"

"Was it? When was this?"

"Two or three years ago."

"Then who was the man I interviewed, two days ago?"

"I've no idea, constable." He handed her a second photograph of the same man but older; she took it.

"What about this one? He's the man I interviewed."

She glanced at the picture and said, "Don't know him, officer."

"Didn't she have any other friends besides you?"

"No, she kept to herself."

"What did she study?"

"English, You?"

"I left college. Is that all officer?"

"No, could you come down to the station and make a statement?"

"What, now I'm last for work?"

No matter what the outcome was, he wanted to solve the case and would do whatever it took, to find this person who did this to his girl.

That weekend He sat in his flat, dressed in light blue striped pyjamas. 'When' 'the phone rang', 'he picked it up and spoke, "Hello, who's this?"

"Good morning, Tyler," said a pleasing voice.

"Hold on a minute, the Inspector is on the line, and he'd like a word with you."

"Ah, Tyler!"

"' Yes, what can I do for you, sir?"

"I've heard you've retaken a day off."

"Yes, I am not well, sir."

"Did I get you out of bed, did I?"

"Yes, you did. I'm sick, sir."

"Yes, pull the other it's got bells on, you're not sick, are you? I know what you're up ''to. You're investigating the death of your ex-girlfriend, aren't you? Will you be in tomorrow?"

"Goodbye, sir," Tyler put the phone down.

Afterwards, he remembered his phone conversation from the other day with the girl, about the man she'd seen at the time of her death, but who was he and where can he find him?

Later that day, Tyler left the flat and saw a man getting out of his four-door, red sedan car with white stripes across the bonnet, carrying something over his right shoulder, wrapped in a carpet and wondered what was going on.

Tyler shouted across to him. "Oi you, Mr! Stop where you are! I want to talk to you about the body you just threw in the river!" But he took to his heels and like a bat out of hell, he ran off, sticking his two fingers up to the constable.

"Up your copper, you couldn't catch a rat!"

After dark, the suspect returned to the crime scene where he'd left his car, jumped into it and drove away.

Tyler, a slow thinking copper who never spent much time in school, liked a drink or two, sometimes when he was off duty, he'd treat himself to a single malt whiskey and listened to Handel's *The Water Music Suites,* one to three that took him to happier times when he met Tara. His biggest regret was that he didn't marry her when he should have. "Farewell, my love, for you were my only real love. You will ''be missed, my love."

He leaned back in his brown leather, office chair; thinking of her, and there beside him was a single malt whiskey. It was his day off. He sat there and thought. *She just lay there stiff as a board; she must've been dead at least an hour before I found her body*.

The phone rang, the Inspector nodded to Tyler, who walked over to the desk, picked up the recycler and listened for a moment or two, then placed his hand over the mouthpiece.

"It's for you, sir. There's a young blonde woman on the line. She was here the other day and wants to speak to you about someone giving her a black eye the other night, when she came out of the Juliet pub, sir."

"Tell her I'll see her in my office later this afternoon."

"Right, sir."

He put the phone down, sat on the desk and thought about the case and crimes some people tried getting away ''with. 'This played on his mind, and he couldn't sleep. He got up and walked on the floor all night thinking, *'it's got to be someone that had known her, but who; and why my girl? 'If I get my hands on him, I'll kill him!*

That took him back to the days when he was on the wrong side of the law and got in with the crazy people until Uncle

Tommy came along and put his thought. College helped him on his way to a better idea of life.

He thought of himself as Perry Mason, but after his father, was killed, he changed his mind and became a police officer. He left college in 1997 and went to Hendon Police College and graduated with full honour.

'This was when things were good and all he had to think about then, was what he is having for his tea when he gets home from College and couldn't wait to get into the house to put the TV on.

DCI Peter Dean Corbett pulled into the car park and parked his gold vintage Bentley: a man in his late 40s with dark black hair, white sideboards, wearing brown NHS spectacles, a no-nonsense person who did everything by the book, but if things didn't go right, he'd go mad and do his nut. He had a nose for crime and an eye for art. He could spot a fake, a mile off when he saw one or a con artist.

With his right hand, he brushed his hair back and said to him, "I fancy a drink." But he didn't drink on duty, a hard-working copper with a caseload of files of unsolved crimes that were piling up on his desk looking at him.

George Charles Malcolm ''was never caught: a master forger that they'd nicknamed 'The Tiger' because left the places as he found it.

No one could catch him; he was that good. His forged paintings looked real, and his letters were so perfect that the police couldn't tell the difference between the real and fake

Corbett, a very knowledgeable person, who knew his Mozart and Handel in his youth. He'd listen to those composers, but as he grew older, he preferred to listen to Jazz music on Jazz FM

An intellectual person who wouldn't let anyone get the better of him, with his tough-talking and hard looks. He could tell when they lied to him. Before he was a police officer, he had worked as a Docker during the day at Wilmot's shipyard and night. He'd stepped into the ring as a prize-fighter and always won his fights.

In the ring, he 'was known as Sugar Ray Corbett. He retired from the ring because of his opponent Sidney Leonard Knight, who died after going fourteen rounds. It was a fixed fight. The referee Edward Jimmy Featherstone ''was paid to turn a blind eye and take a bribe.

'This delayed his promotion; the inquiry exonerated him from blame. After this, Cobbett wouldn't fight again; even when people pushed him, he'd walk away and put in for a transfer to another force.

He was born in a Manchester ghetto on 25 February 1960, the year of rock and roll music scene, but grew up in a council house in Westhampton.

Cobbett, the second son of factory workers, who 'were educated at the Barker Secondary School in Formby Street, Westhampton, studied the three 'R's, English Literature and history.

When he 'was a child his father' 'Bernard, was between jobs, until he won £50m on the pools, bought his own company called Corbett Industries. He ran the company until his death on 3 September 1972, aged 49 from a diabetic stroke due to alcohol and being a chain smoker.

His mother Hilda, a casual smoker, worked in an enamel factory as an enamel platter during the day and at night, she worked as a school cleaner until she died from a heart attack on 22 December 1989, aged 66.

His brother Norman Stanley was born on 31 January 1957 and had a severe learning disability; through him, father smashing his head against the landing wall when he was a child and spent eighteen years of his life in little more homes for the severely disabled people, where he fought with another resident, Larry Albrecht Ewing. It 'was later demolished in 2000. He shared the flat with him at the time, pushed him down a flight of stairs and accused him of telling tales about his brother claimed that he didn't care a damn about him.

Now he lives in sheltered accommodation at High Green Close. In 2010, he suffered a severe stroke. He 'was admitted to the infirmary. Three years later, he 'was exposed to Snow

Trees, a Psychiatric Hospital for patients with learning disabilities.

He started to suffer from hallucinations and insomnia, saying that he could see images of dead people walking around, passing blood from his urine. Corbett received a phone call while on a case, but he never had enough time to see his brother because of his job.

Corbett ''was dressed in a ceramic white shirt, dark greyish suit with a black bow tie, a red carnation in his left lapel, a white hankie in his top pocket and his hand. And in his hand, he carried a cane with a gold handle, wore a bowler hat with a Belgian moustache.

In his spare time, he wrote art reviews for a magazine. His family were historians and were part of the gentry. 'A self-made millionaire, who now owned Corbett Industries: made microchips for computers, video parts for digital TVs.

He was also an amateur poet, who wrote poetry that had '; been published. Two of his favourite poets were William Shakespeare (1564-1616) and John Donne (1572-1631).

He quoted a verse from each one:

"Shall I compare thee to a summer's day? Thou art lovelier and more moderate rough winds do shake the darling buds of May." – Shakespeare

"Busy old fool, unruly sun; why dost thou thus, through windows and curtains call on us?" – John Donne

"There you are, Sergeant, that's poetry, my son."

"Not my cup of tea, sir."

"You read it not drink it, Serge."

His wife, Mrs Brenda Paula Corbett, ran the company. Her maiden name was Jarvis.

A working-class, prickly and unpopular person with a no-nonsense approach to life; she'd met Corbett through an investigation where both of her parents 'were' killed in an arson attack on that tragic day on 16 June 1977.

When she returned home late after a college reunion party with her friends, she found the house had 'been' burnt down to the ground and the cat called Sid, a family pet, with its throat cut.

She couldn't understand why her family was hated in this way and why they were singled out. They were victims of a hate campaign and had been sent hate mail with death threats and bricks through their windows.

People thought they were Germans. She was born in Austria; her childhood memories were of her father taking her fishing on weekends at the Watson River when she was just four-years-old.

She'd walked past there each day and stood on the bank, thought of her father 'who used to fish a lot', but he never courts anything. Her sister, Jessie, had committed suicide by slitting her own throat, and her brother Douglas, was confined to a mental asylum, where he died.

The news around that same year saw the deaths of four famous people: **Elvis Presley, Bing Crosby, Marc Bolan— the frontman of T-Rex—and Maria Callas, an opera singer** – *The case of the Yorkshire Ripper.*

"I would've liked to have worked on that case. I would've caught ''him no trouble, couldn't do better than those who tried."

"I suppose you would've caught him the first time, sir."

"We'll need to know; will we, Sergeant, why someone like him does bad things like that?"

Corbett was fairer to women than he was to men because they were the more equal sexes and did what he could to help them. He had compassion for those women and was lenient with them.

He remembered his childhood; sitting on the stairs, listening to his parents arguing, opening the door, and finding his mother lying on the floor with two black eyes, crying, and never forgot this, or where he came, 'from.

'This is where the human side of Corbett came in juggling between family and his job, 'a man who came up through the ranks and had to make it to the top, the law was his life, and he wasn't going to let anyone stand in his way of getting the top job.

"This is my job, and no one is going to take it from me. I'm on my way to the top, and no one is going to stand in my way. I'll do what it takes, within the law, to get this job."

He got on better with women than men. His male friends always hurt him with their sly remarks about his wealthy lifestyle. A wine drinker, who knew which wines went with meat and fish.

Tyler returned to the station that day; Inspector Corbett entered the office, walked over to the desk where Tyler sat. The Inspector approached the counter and spoke to him.

"What you doing here? I thought I told you; you're off this case! Now go home. Didn't you hear me?"

"I'm investigating the Slater murder, sir."

"No, you're not, because you and she had a love affair five years ago, didn't you?"

"Yes, but she left me for another man."

"Was it Stones?"

"I don't know, sir. The affair was over a year before she was found dead. He killed her, sir! He had a motive and an opportunity, because he knew her," his characteristic mood was flat as the bear he dank, it never changed.

'He drove the same car and wore the same jacket with the same hat, all year round in all weathers, each time we saw him.

"So did you. There's no proof; he' the one who committed this offence. The witnesses are too frightened to give evidence against him, and the evidence disappeared along with the witnesses, or they turned up dead if they couldn't pay him."

"I'd stay away from him' 'if I were you. He doesn't care if you a copper or not, he'll kill you anyway! You get to find him before he finds you!"

"But he did it, sir. I know he did it, sir."

"But each time we got close to catching him, he had an alibi and always got away with it."

"Not this time, sir, he won't."

"That case is closed, constable! Your predecessors, DS Henderson and Constable Sharon Taylor, worked on the evidence before you did and they too thought that they could convict him of murdering two schoolgirls: Lorraine Whither aged 15, an Afro-Caribbean, carried a handbag and 13-year-old Asian Noreen Batty she carried a darkish blue briefcase.

Both girls wore school uniforms on the day they went missing on a Friday in January 1969, while on their way home from school. At the time of the investigation, a set of footprints were found at the crime scene, besides their bodies."

"Who are they?"

"They were abducted by a hooded person, who drove a pale-coloured Land Rover car with the windows blacked out so no one can see who is inside but the people inside, can see you."

"Did anyone see the car, sir?"

"Yes, a Gardner truck driver saw the car approaching from the other side of the road and signalled to it to stop, but it carried on."

"Was it a man or woman driving?"

"We don't know that."

"Is the Truck Company listed in the phone book?"

"No, there's nothing listed under Gardner Trucks."

"We've got to find that truck driver, sir, and ask him or her, if they saw something or someone on the day of the murder, sir."

"Well, get on the phone and find out where that truck stop is."

"But there are lots of them, and it'll take all day, sir."

"Seeing someone tonight, are you?"

"No, sir."

"Well, get on with it."

"Yes, sir."

The following day, Inspector Corbett and the forensic team arrived at the scene where Tara's body lay, while the doctor's team placed her body into a body bag and zipped it up, they carried it out into the street and put it into a black van, and drove away.

Corbett drove his car to the morgue and arrived at the lab. He walked in through the door, approached the doctor and asked her, "Was it murder, doctor?"

"Yes."

"How?"

"She was suffocated with a flannelette pillow, Inspector."

"When, what time did she die?"

'Two days ago, between the hours of 10.00 and 11.00, Inspector."

"Was she raped, doctor?"

"There's no sign of sexual activity. Do you know who, 'her father is, Inspector?"

"No, who is he?"

"He's only Jack Slater, a government minister – the victim never regained consciousness." Doctor Crawford examined the body.

She removed her clothing during the examination. She discovered whip marks on the victim's back.

The doctor examined them and found five deep cuts between the victim's shoulder blades. She covered the body with the sheet and sat at her desk in deep thought, then spoke to him again, "Who's going to tell her father?"

Inspector Peter Dean Corbett was leaving the lab when the doctor called him back. He returned to the lab room and spoke to the doctor, "Yes."

"You wanted to see me again."

The doctor pulled back the sheet. "Yes. Look at this, Inspector."

"What are those marks on her back?"

"She was whipped with a horsewhip or with a riding crop. I found these love letters in the victim's coat pocket."

"Whose are they?"

"You're not going to like it, Inspector."

"Don't play games doctor; just tell me whose are they?"

"They're Tyler's, Inspector."

"Where's Tyler! Where is he? He's never here when I need him! Oh, there you are: I've been looking for you. Drinking on duty, are you?" he joked.

"No, I was up all night thinking about the case and who could have done it. What do you want, sir?"

"I'll see you in my office tomorrow at 9.00 sharp to see the Chief."

"Right, sir!"

"And don't be late." But the following morning, Tyler arrived at the chief's office fifteen minutes late and walked up to a short flight of stairs and knocked on the office door.

A voice shouted. "So, you finally made it have you? Come in! Where have you been? 'You' were supposed to be here at 9:00!"

"I overslept, sir."

"Last night investigating, you mean!"

"What do you want, sir?"

"The doctor found some of your love letters on Miss Slater's body. Do these letters belong to you?"

"Yes, they're mine, sir. Have you read them, sir?"

"Yes, I'm conducting a murder inquiry, not the London Philharmonic Orchestra, they're part of the murder inquiry."

"But they're private, sir. How would you like it if I read yours?"

"We're investigating a murder. We don't have time to play games now get on with it!"

The Inspector handed Tyler the original copies.

"You can keep those, constables. I've photocopied them."

Tyler left the chief's office with the original copies of his love letters and walked back to the bus station, later that day. He saw a gang of punk rockers throwing stones at the same bus shelter window.

The gang had run off and left a youth standing there: a boy, Tyler knew from his past, as the boy turned his head and saw a constable approach him, he started running. Tyler shouted.

"Hey, you stop that! That's vandalism! Come back here. I want a word with you!" But when Ken saw the constable, he ran through the bus terminal.

Tyler chased him through Westhampton Bus Terminal and had him cornered between two buses. Caught him and grabbed him by his shirt collar, pushed him up against the frosty bus shelter window and questioned him about the murder of Tara.

"Tell me who killed Miss Slater!"

"Not me copper, I didn't kill her!"

"No, but you know who did, don't you; you're always hugging about the street arts, you!"

"No, I'm not, and I'm no grass, copper! Go and find out for yourself!"

"On your way and don't let me catch you hang around here again or I'll nick you next time!"

"Sod off, copper! I'll tell my father about you!"

"You can tell whom you like! Just go home and get out of my sight before I'll take you in and you'll spend a night in a cell-like your uncle, Sidney, a member of your family who did some years go for driving without a license when they were younger!"

"You do, and I'll stick a knife in you!"

"If you do that, sonny, you'll be in serious trouble, and you'll do time in Wormwood Scrubs for murdering a police officer."

"Do you know who my father is?!"

"No, I don't. I've no idea. 'Who is 'he?' Prince Charles, is he?"

"Nah, he's an MP!"

"What does that stand for? Military Police?"

"No, he's a Member of Parliament, you daft twit!"

"Well I don't know, do I? I'm just an average street copper, and I'm unable to put the clues together myself. I'm not CID. They're the superintendent's blue-eyed boys."

"They are, but we're the ones who must tell some poor sod that a member of their family, sons, daughters, etc. have either been shot or stabbed. Those flat feet, in CID, take all the glory. Those bloody glory, boys!"

He sent the boy home with a flea in his ear. At about 4.00 that same afternoon, Tyler had left Bridgewater Police Station because Sergeant Coombes had sent him home when he received a report from a distraught Mrs Yvonne Roach about Tyler, who had caught her son, Ken, and a gang of youths, In the early hours of the morning, throwing stones at a West Midlands bus station window.

She claimed that Constable Tyler had assaulted her son by giving him a clip around his ear hole. The Sergeant turned to the boy and asked him.

"Is this true, son? I don't think that Constable Tyler would do a thing like that he doesn't hit children."

"Yes, he did. He beat me up in the street!"

"He caught you and the other boys hanging around a murder scene spraying graffiti all over the window, didn't he, son?"

"No, I wasn't!"

"Then why did you run?"

"I don't like coppers!"

"Tyler."

"Yes, sir."

"A word, please. Do you know this boy?"

"Yes, I know the vandal."

"That'll do, constable."

"I caught him and his mates vandalising Westhampton Bus Station, sir. I pushed him up against the glass window and questioned him about it. Is that all, sir? I've got to go; I am late for a date."

"No, you don't, did you assault him, constable?"

"No, I didn't, sir."

"He claimed you did."

"He's a liar; he threatened to cut me with a knife."

The sergeant turned to the boy again.

"Did you, son?"

"No, it wasn't me, the other boys told me to do it!"

The sergeant asked,

"Which other boys and where are they now?"

Tyler turned towards the boy and spoke,

"Yes, it was you. I caught you brandishing a single-bladed knife. You were going to stab me with it, weren't you?"

The boy's mother turned to him and said.

"Wait 'til I get you home! You're not seeing those boys again! Do you hear it? 'You're confined to barracks!"

"This isn't the army, ma!"

"Don't you be cheeky; you're just like your father; he was always in trouble when he was your age! You give this family a bad name!"

As she was leaving the station with her son, Tyler approached her.

"Excuse me, madam; who's going to pay for the window?"

"Not me!"

She smacked Ken across his head.

"Shut it; he wasn't asking you and get in the bloody car! Your father's a Tory MP for God's sake! The press will have a field day. I can see the headlines, '*MP's son threatens copper with a knife*', now get in the car and shut up!"

"But Ma, I didn't do it, the other boys did it."

She walked out the door and down the steps to the car park; got in her car, a yellow four-door Peugeot 1.5 and drove off.

Later that day, Tyler left Bridgewater Station; he walked down the lane, turned left into the bus station.

He turned his head and heard a newspaper seller, shouting, "Bus shelter murder, read all about it; Police baffled – a mad killer on the loose!" He approached the seller.

"Here, give us one of those papers, mate."

"That'll be 50p, sir." He handed over a 50p coin.

"Thank you, sir. Cold, isn't it? Have a good day now."

"A good day, indeed! It's all right for him. He doesn't have to catch the killer, he stands in the red box all day long, just selling newspapers. That's his job that all the dune!"

He bought a copy of the Express and Star newspaper with a giant headline splashed on the front page: BUS SHELTER

MURDER and sighed, "Humph! Look at the headline. Who the hell's doing those murders?"

He walked back to the bus station; he turned to page four; the headline stood out and stared at him. DEATH AT THE HANDS OF A KILLER! He joined a small bus queue and heard two people arguing.

Tyler was on his way home when he witnessed an argument between Jackie Cline; a sex worker and Charles Gold Pen an out-of-work banker that embezzled money from customers' accounts and, was sacked for stealing.

Tyler approached them and decided to investigate the row himself when he saw Gold Pen slap, Miss Cline, across her face.

He spoke to him, "I saw that, sir! Stop that at once! That's an assault! I'll have to arrest you for that, sir!"

.An ambitious copper who wanted to make commissionaire by the time he reached fifty.

"You can try copper!"

"Oh, hello, don't I know you? Aren't you Charles Reginald Gold Pen? Haven't you been in prison for being a curb-crawler and selling dodgy cars? A bit of an Arthur Daley, aren't we sir? Didn't I see you at the station the other day?"

"No, it wasn't me, copper!"

"We have your criminal record on the file back at the station. It's as long as your arm! Interesting bedtime reading! That's a coincidence that both of you are arguing at the same bus shelter, where the body of a 25-year-old female student, was found dead, three days ago. Do you know anything about Miss Slater's murder, do you? Didn't you have a relationship with her some time ago?"

"Yes, but she ended the affair. It wasn't me, copper!"

"A tie was found beside her body. Have you lost one, sir?"

"No, I haven't! What's it got to do with you?"

"Don't tell lies, sir. We have a witness who saw you both last week at a derelict housing estate. You paid her for sex, and two days later, she, was found murdered. Did you rape her, then kill her? Because you were, seen running away from there, sir."

"Prove it, copper!"

Tyler was about to push Gold Pen's face up against the bus station window when he 'heard a voice' in the background, saying, "What do you think you're doing? That'll do, constable! As from now, you're on leave! Now go home!"

'Give me five minutes alone with him and to question him, sir. Can't you see, he knows something about the murder?"

"Don't you speak to me in that tone of voice, or you'll find yourself unemployed."

"I might as well for the use I am!"

"What was that?"

"Nothing, sir. I'm going down to the pub."

"No, you're not. What is your connection with the victim? Didn't you have a relationship with her some time ago?"

"Yes, but it was over five years ago. We were going to be married, but on that day, she disappeared."

"That's a coincidence, isn't it, constable? That she disappeared on the actual day you were both going to be married."

As he walked away, the Inspector spoke, "Oi! I'm talking to you, constable! Now, where's he gone? If he's gone to find her killer, he'll get himself killed."

Corbett drove back to the lab and walked across to the car park and up the small steps, pushed open the glass door and walked over to the table and spoke to the doctor. "Hello, doctor. Any results yet?"

"Not yet. I haven't finished the post-mortem."

"Any idea when?"

"Later on today, Inspector, the press will be all over this case and will want to know why no one is doing anything finding this killer, Inspector."

"We've no idea who's doing this doctor; have you?"

"No, I've not."

As they arrived at the morgue, the press was outside, waiting, and hounded the Inspector. "Inspector, could you tell us whether it is true that you sit at home, listening to music and drinking wine, while the other officers search for this maniac who's murdering those women?"

"No comment! It's not a crime to like beautiful things. Get away from here. 'This is private property. You're trespassing."

The Inspector was about to leave the lab when his eyes glanced at the doctor's laboratory assistant Paul Midfield, a five-foot-six male with light brown hair, who was sitting at the desk, reading a copy of The Metro newspaper. The headline read.

INSPECTOR RELAXES AT HOME LISTENS TO MUSIC AND DRINKS WINE, WHILE ALL OTHER OFFICERS WORKED AROUND THE CLOCK SEARCHING FOR THE KILLER.

He left through the door and muttered, "Don't believe everything you read in newspapers, or what you see on the TV news."

Charles was the prime suspect for the murder of the 'Duchess' Sarah Gold Pen.' This was her nickname because of the red hair and the features of the Duchess of York.

Charles was charged with her murder, but when questioned about her death, he denied it.

"I didn't bloody kill her, coppers! You should be out there catching those real criminals and not picking on innocent people like us!"

"You're not innocent. You've been inside for curb-crawling, haven't you, sir?"

Inspector Gerry Callahan of the Flying Squad, a white male in his late 50s is wearing a dark-grey suit and a light-blue denim shirt, with brown suede shoes.

His sidekick Detective Sgt Sheila Wallace, a Filipino, thin-faced woman in her mid-thirties, stood five-ten with chestnut brown eyes, brownish shoulder-length hair, wore a black and white catsuit, expensive silver transition lenses with a yellow t-shirt.

They'd been called in by the top Boss to investigate the Gold Pen murder.